The Birthday Present

Written by Susannah Reed

Illustrated by Fran and David Brylewski

Collins

Who and what is in this story?

Listen and say

Download the audio at www.collins.co.uk/839828

present

lock

message

clue

2125

🎧 It was Matt's birthday. His friends Paul and Kim were at his house.

"Happy Birthday, Matt!" they said.
"What do you want for your birthday?"

"I'd like a new bike," said Matt. "I love riding my bike, but my old bike is very small. I need a new one."

"Good idea." said Paul.

Kim smiled and looked out of the window.

"Look, Matt!" she said. "There's a big present in your garden."

"What is it?" asked Matt. "Is it a bike?"

"I don't know," said Kim, "But it's very big."

"Open it and let's see," said Paul.

Matt went into the garden and opened the present. He took out a very small message.

Oh!

What does the message say?

"Go to your bedroom and take a look," Matt read. "I'm hiding behind your favourite book."

"It's a clue," said Paul.

"Yes," said Matt. "Let's go and look!"

The children ran to the bookcase in
Matt's bedroom.

"This is my favourite book!" said Matt.

"And there's a present," said Kim.

Matt picked up the present.

"It's square," he said. "It isn't a bike. Is it a basketball?"

"Open it and let's see," said Kim.

Matt opened the present. He took out a small box.

"It isn't a basketball," said Paul. "Is it a camera?"

"I don't know," said Matt. "I can't open the box."

"Look," said Matt. "We need the numbers for this lock."

"Yes," said Kim. "But what are they?"

"Let's read this message," said Paul.

"Eyes, nose, ears, then add the numbers!" read Paul. "What does that mean?"

"I know!" said Matt. "It's a number clue."

Eyes, nose, ears, then add the numbers.

"Two eyes, one nose, two ears, then add – that's five," said Matt.

"You're right," said Kim. "Let's try 2125."

Matt tried the numbers and the lock opened.

Matt took a small thing out of the box.
He held it up.

"It's a key," he said. "And there's one
more clue."

"What does it say?" asked Kim.

"Open a door with this key," read Paul.
"It's in the garden. Can you see?"

"A door in the garden!" said Matt.
"I know!"

The children ran out to the garden.
Matt put the key into the door of
the garden room. The door opened.

"What can you see?" asked Kim.

"I can see Mum and Dad," said Matt. "And a bike! I can see a beautiful, new bike!"

The children went into the room.
Matt's mum gave him a message.

Happy Birthday
from Mum, Dad,
Kim and Paul!

The message read, "Happy Birthday from
Mum, Dad, Kim and Paul!"

"Wow!" said Matt! "What a fantastic present!"

"And you knew?" he said to Paul and Kim.

"Yes," they said. "We wrote the clues."

"Thank you!" said Matt.

Picture dictionary

Listen and repeat

bookcase

clue

idea

lock

Happy Birthday from Mum, Dad, Kim and Paul!

message

pick up

smile

1 Look and order the story

2 Listen and say

Collins

Published by Collins
An imprint of HarperCollins*Publishers*
Westerhill Road
Bishopbriggs
Glasgow
G64 2QT

HarperCollins *Publishers*
Macken House,
39/40 Mayor Street Upper,
Dublin 1
D01 C9W8
Ireland

William Collins' dream of knowledge for all began with the publication of his first book in 1819.

A self-educated mill worker, he not only enriched millions of lives, but also founded a flourishing publishing house. Today, staying true to this spirit, Collins books are packed with inspiration, innovation and practical expertise. They place you at the centre of a world of possibility and give you exactly what you need to explore it.

© HarperCollins*Publishers* Limited 2020

10 9 8 7 6 5 4 3 2 1

ISBN 978-0-00-839828-6

Collins® and COBUILD® are registered trademarks of HarperCollins*Publishers* Limited

www.collins.co.uk/elt

British Library Cataloguing in Publication Data

A catalogue record for this publication is available from the British Library.

Author: Susannah Reed
Illustrator: Fran and David Brylewski (Beehive)
Series editor: Rebecca Adlard
Commissioning editor: Zoë Clarke
Publishing manager: Lisa Todd
Product managers: Jennifer Hall and Caroline Green
In-house editor: Alma Puts Keren
Project manager: Emily Hooton
Editor: Frances Amrani
Proofreaders: Natalie Murray and Michael Lamb
Cover designer: Kevin Robbins
Typesetter: 2Hoots Publishing Services Ltd
Audio produced by id audio, London
Reading guide author: Emma Wilkinson
Production controller: Rachel Weaver
Printed and bound by: Pureprint, UK

Download the audio for this book and a reading guide for parents and teachers at www.collins.co.uk/839828